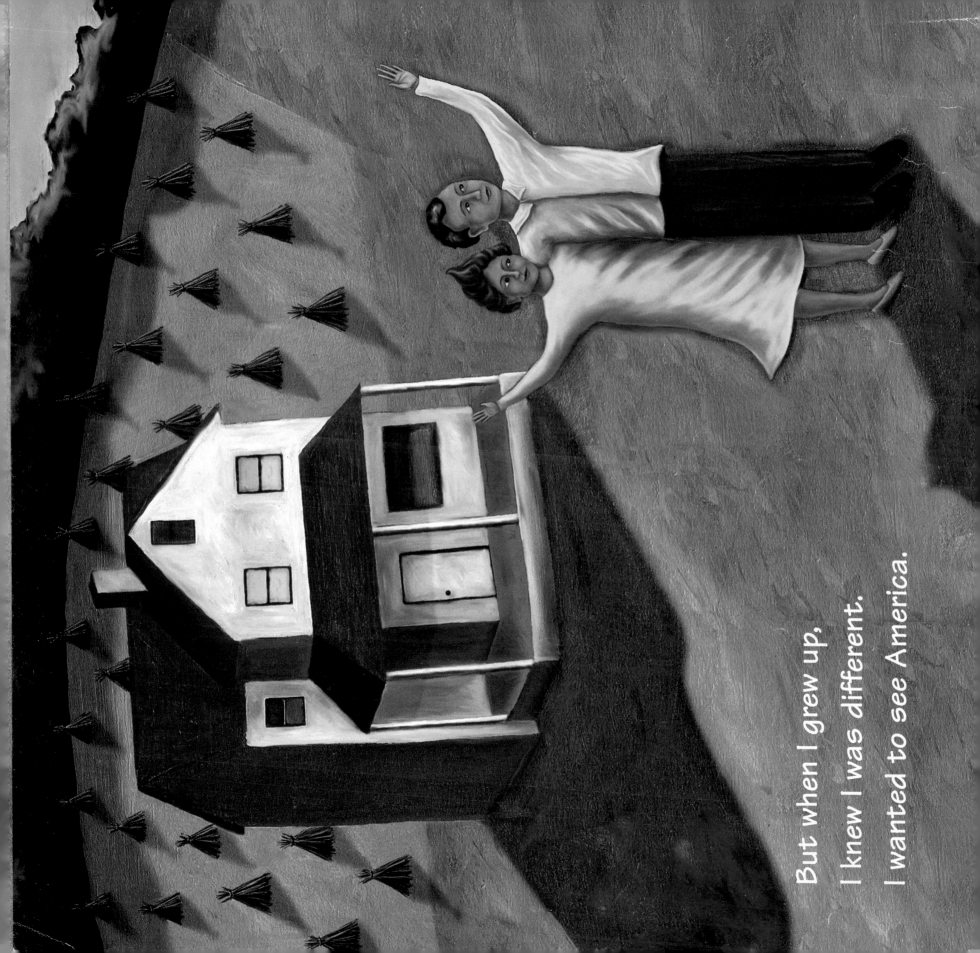

But when I grew up,
I knew I was different.
I wanted to see America.

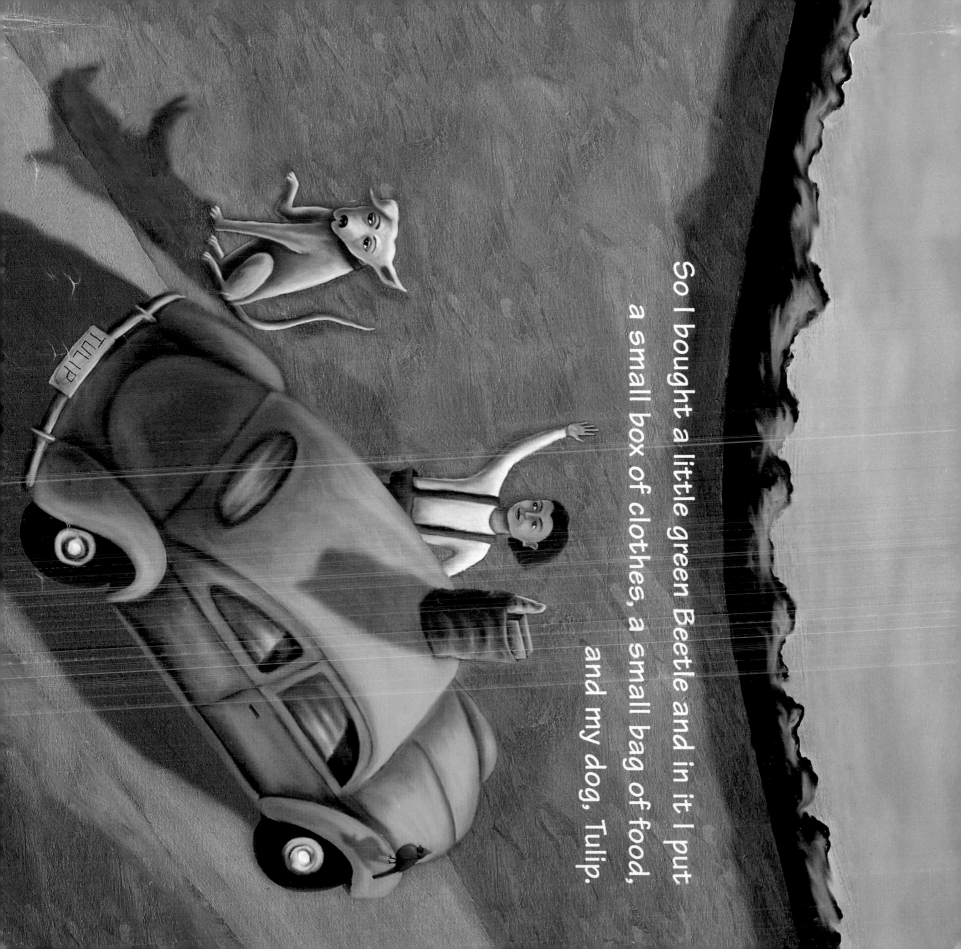

So I bought a little green Beetle and in it I put a small box of clothes, a small bag of food, and my dog, Tulip.

And we left Ohio
and went across America.

This is what we saw:

The farms in Iowa. They are pictures:
White houses. Red roofs.

Green, green rolling hills and black garden soil all around them.

Farms like castles in a fairyland,
serene in the morning fog.

There are no farms like Iowa's.

The skies in Nebraska.

They are everything.

They are vast and dark and low and ominous.

And a tiny Beetle feels even tinier,

driving beneath them.

It feels a little afraid.

The wind in Wyoming.
Everything flaps.

Tulip's ears flapped all the way across Wyoming.
And when we stopped to get out of the Beetle,
the wind filled our noses and watered our eyes
and Tulip was ready to get back into the car.

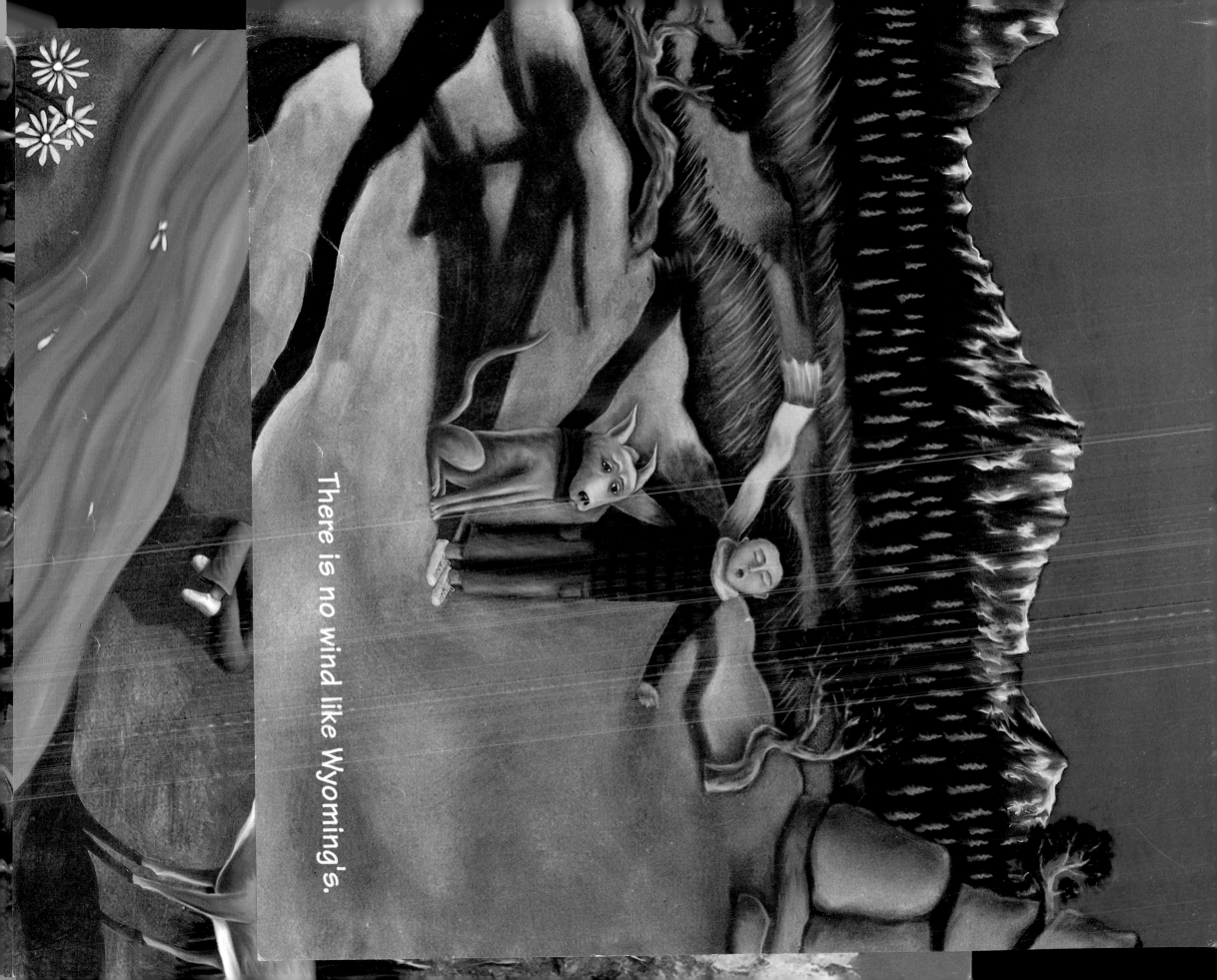

There is no wind like Wyoming's.

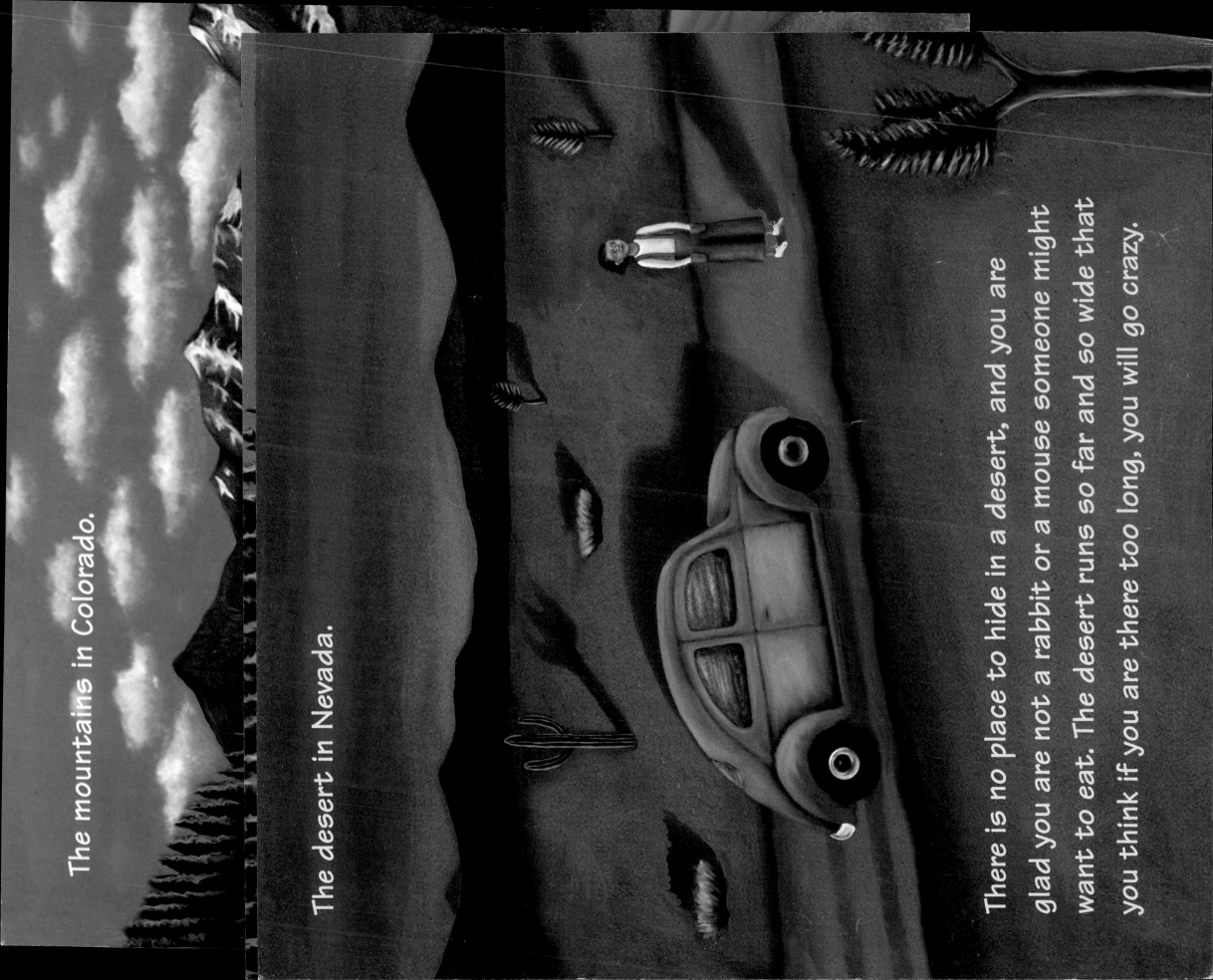

The mountains in Colorado.

The desert in Nevada.

There is no place to hide in a desert, and you are glad you are not a rabbit or a mouse someone might want to eat. The desert runs so far and so wide that you think if you are there too long, you will go crazy.

Its flowers are strange and beautiful, and
Tulip chased salamanders between its rocks.

Tulip and I did silly things
we would do only in Nevada.

I took all my clothes off.

I don't know why.
Because no one was there.

Tulip wasn't as silly.

She just dug a big hole for no reason.

There is no desert like Nevada's.

The ocean in Oregon.

You drive up a winding mountain road

and you think there is no ocean anywhere.

You drive between a stand of firs

and you think: no ocean.

Then you blink, and there it is: